Alphabets for Calligraphers Letterers and Graphic Designers

Kaye E. Frost

Angus&Robertson
An imprint of HarperCollins*Publishers*

For all the aspiring calligraphers and letterers I've taught who, like "Oliver", still want more, ...here it is...

more!

Every effort has been made to contact the owners of copyright. The publishers would welcome any further information regarding copyright ownership.

An Angus & Robertson Publication

Angus&Robertson, an imprint of
HarperCollins*Publishers*
25 Ryde Road, Pymble, Sydney, NSW 2073, Australia
31 View Road, Glenfield, Auckland 10, New Zealand
77-85 Fulham Palace Road, London W6 8JB, United Kingdom
10 East 53rd Street, New York NY 10022, USA

First published in Australia in 1994

Copyright © Kaye E. Frost 1994

This book is copyright.
Apart from any fair dealing for the purposes of private study, research, criticism or review, as permitted under the Copyright Act, no part may be reproduced by any process without written permission. Inquiries should be addressed to the publishers.

National Library of Australia
Cataloguing-in-Publication data:

Frost, Kaye. E.
Alphabets for calligraphers, letterers & graphic designers.

ISBN 0 207 18417 8.

I. Alphabets. 2. Calligraphy. 3. Lettering. I. Title.
745.61

Printed in Hong Kong

9 8 7 6 5 4 3 2 1
97 96 95 94

Table of Contents

Introduction	1
Calligraphic Alphabets	3
Directories	4
Alphabets	8
Applications	43
Ready Reference to Line Heights	50
Calligraphic Societies	52
Alphabets for Brushes and Felt Pens	53
Introduction to Felt Pens	54
Examples of Markers and Brushes	57
Directories	60
Alphabets	62
Applications	91
Recommended Books	99
Suppliers	100

The Moving Finger writes; and having writ, Moves on :

'RUBAIYAT OF OMAR KHAYYAM'

Introduction

Most of us underestimate or overlook what an impact the written word has on our everyday life. Just in the course of a single day we encounter it on almost everything we look at. Books, computers, packaging, signs, television and magazines. It can teach us, instruct us, direct us, warn us, even entertain us. The development of our alphabet is a fascinating subject to study. It is estimated that there are some 4000 languages spoken in the world today, many having perished. Not all alphabets have the letter shapes we are familiar with. It is easy to see why some folk have trouble trying to communicate with others from foreign places.

WRITING:
is when letters are written directly with a pen, pencil, brush, any writing tool. There is little or no need to retouch them.

LETTERING:
is when letters are carefully drawn, that is constructed with a pencil, corrected, filled in with ink or paint then retouched if needed.

TYPE:
is when letterforms are first designed by lettering, then cast in metal or photographed for exact duplication when finally printed.

Hence

- **WRITING:** Calligraphy
  - Direct brushwork eg script
  - Felt pens

- **LETTERING:** Ticketwriting
  - Signwriting

- **TYPE (or fonts):** Letraset / Rapitype / Geotype etc.
  - Desktop publishing

WRITING TOOLS:

PENS: TICKETWRITING NIBS / CALLIGRAPHY NIBS
- FELT PENS / BALLPOINTS / FIBRE-TIP
- TECHNICAL DRAWING PENS (*Architectural*)
- AUTOMATIC PENS
- COIT PENS
- FOUNTAIN PENS

BRUSHES: TICKETWRITING / SIGNWRITING (*chisel or pointed*)

PENCILS: GRAPHITE / COLOURED / WATER-SOLUBLE

OTHER: PASTELS / CRAYONS / CHALK / QUILLS
- SPONGE BRUSHES / REED PENS
- BAMBOO PENS / TONGUE DEPRESSOR

COLOUR:

INK: WATERCOLOUR / WATERPROOF
- LIGHTFAST or FADEPROOF
- LIMITED LIGHTFASTNESS
- TRANSPARENT / OPAQUE / TRANSLUCENT
- PEARLESCENT / PIGMENTED
- ACRYLIC / FREE FLOWING / NON-CLOGGING

PAINT: PLASTIC / VINYL / ACRYLIC
- GOUACHE (*designer colour*)
- WATERCOLOUR
- ENAMEL (*water-based / solvent based*)

Calligraphic ALPHABETS

Alphabet Directory

NUMERALS IN TOP RIGHT HAND CORNER
OF EACH SHEET INDICATES PAGE NUMBER

DIRECTORIES

Alphabet Directory

Textura — 21
Eabcdefghijklmn
Epqrstuvwxyz

Commonly referred to as 'Old English'. Textura is the most well-known form of Gothic otherwise known as Black Letter. It was developed in the 12th century from Carolingian. (see page 62) which was written greatly compressed.

ABCDEFGH
IJKLMNO
RSTUVW

Gothic Cursive — 22
Here is a lesser known Gothic alphabet.

Eabcdefghijklmnopq
Estuvwxyyz (& ampersand and the)
ABCDEFGHI
LMNOPQRST
VWXYZYZ

The labour of the writer is the refreshing of the reader. The one depletes the body, the other advances the...

Rotunda — 23
Rotunda is a style that evolved from Gothic Script, but is much more rounded, hence its name. It was developed in Spain (13th c.)

Eabcdefghijklmn
opqrstuvwxyz
aoeffgz (Variations of a, d, e, f, g and r)

ABCDEFGHI
JKLMNOPQ
RSTUVWXY
Z variations BDDD
EEHPQR

Rotunda was commonly used in Books of Hours (personal prayerbooks) in gigantic manuscripts for church use and in musical notation.

Schwabacher — 24
Eabcdefghijklmn
Eopqrstuvwxyz

This style was developed in the early 1470's in Germany. It has a much more rugged character than Fraktur or Textura. (see page 50)

ABCDEFGH

Batarde — 25
14th - 16th century.

abcdefghyklm
opqrstuvwxyz
ABCDEF
GHIJKLM
NOPQR

Bastard — 26
A modern version of Gothic from the 16th century.

Eabcdefghijk
Elmnopqrstu
Evwxyz
ABCDEFG
HIJKLMN
PQRST
VWXYZ

Fraktur — 27
This hand is a German develop... It became less popular in the... when pen flourishes and scroll...

Eabcdefghijklm
Eqrstuvwxyz
Eadfghs Variations of lower case

ABCDEFGH
IJKLMNO
PQRSTUV
WXYZS Variation

Pointed Italic — 28
This style has similar features as that of Chancery cursive and Black Letter.

Eabcdefghijklm
Eopqrstuvwxyz
ABCDEFG
HIJKLMN
OPQRSTU
VWXYZ

Pointed Italic can also be written upright. The calligrapher is only concerned with making beautiful forms. ARNOLD BANK

Gothic Numerals — 29
1234567890
1234567890
1234567890

Ampersands et & & &
The ampersand evolved from 'et' the Latin word for 'and'.

& & & & & &
& & & & & &

NUMERALS IN TOP RIGHT HAND CORNER OF EACH SHEET INDICATE PAGE NUMBER

Alphabet Directory

NUMERALS IN TOP RIGHT HAND CORNER
OF EACH SHEET INDICATES PAGE NUMBER

DIRECTORIES

Alphabet Directory

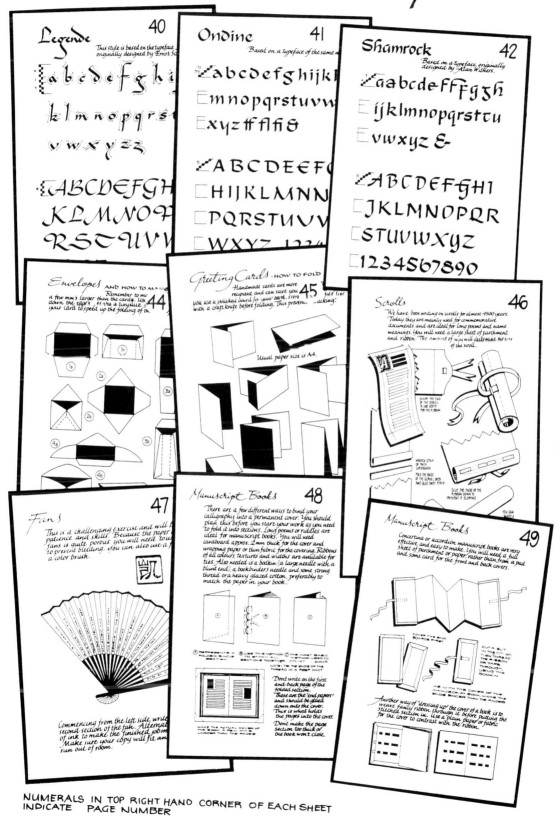

NUMERALS IN TOP RIGHT HAND CORNER OF EACH SHEET INDICATE PAGE NUMBER

DIRECTORIES

Because

this book has been designed as a reference manual, I have arranged the following calligraphic styles as closely as possible to their historical development.

K

UNCIAL 3rd – 9th century

ABCDEFGHIJKL
MNOPQRSTUV
WXYZ EKTU

ABBCDDEFFG
HIJKKLMMN
NOPPQRSTTU
UVWWWXYZ

ABCDEFGHIJK
LMNOPQRSTU
VWXYYZ & &

(this version loosely based on a similar typeface)

1234567890

How to make a serif:

Carolingian

Not all Carolingian is sloped. Uncials or drawn versals were used as capitals.

The club serif (a serif is a stroke which finishes off the end of a letter) is actually formed like this ⌐. This is sometimes hard to do with a steel nib. Use the sequence as above.

Carolingian is smooth, flowing, graceful.

Memorise it well enough to be able to

write it fairly rapidly. The serifs,

once mastered, are quite a delight to

write. Large interlinear spaces essential.

LOMBARDIC INITIALS

ABCDE
FGHIJK
LMNOP
QRSTU
VWXYZ

draw in outline first, then fill in

ALPHABETS

ITALIAN GOTHIC CAPITALS

ALPHABETS

ITALIAN GOTHIC CAPITALS

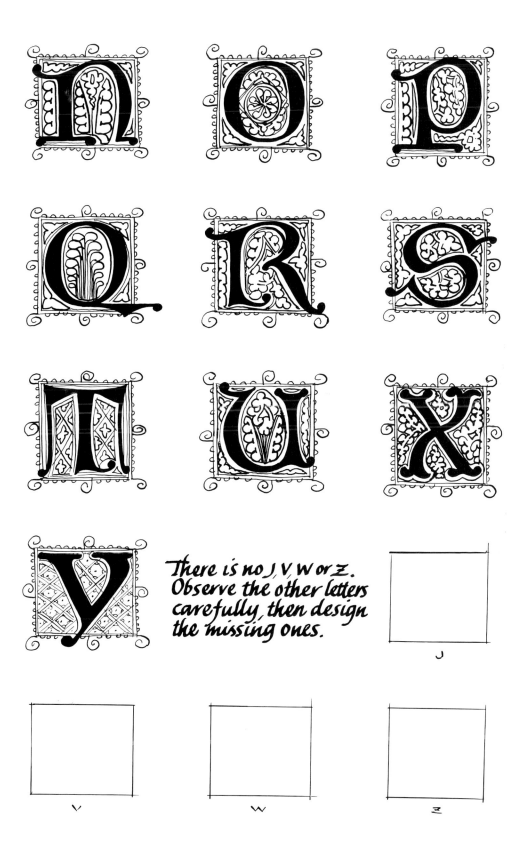

There is no J, V, W or Z. Observe the other letters carefully, then design the missing ones.

ENGLISH INITIALS

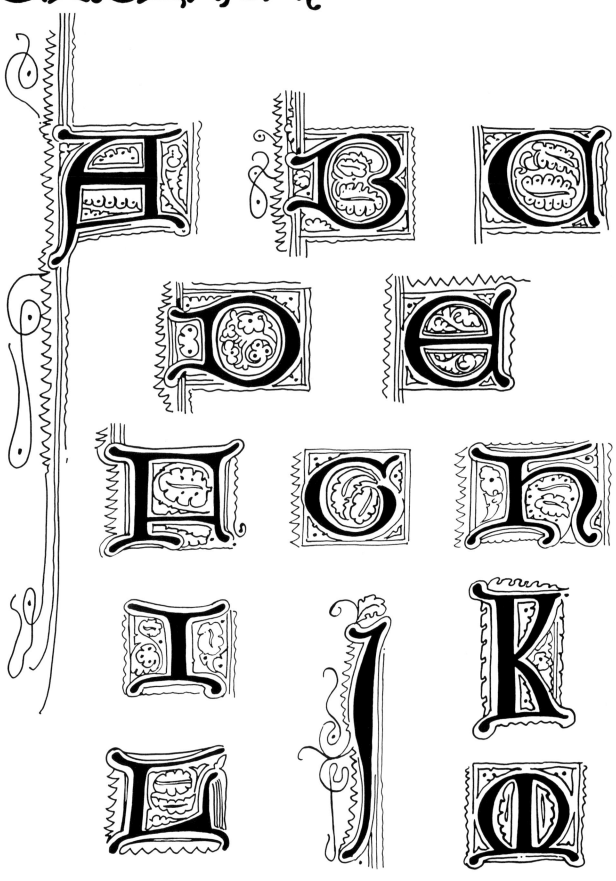

ALPHABETS

ENGLISH INITIALS

Remember to draw in outline first, then fill in.

This set of English initials did not include the letter V.

ALPHABETS

INITIALS

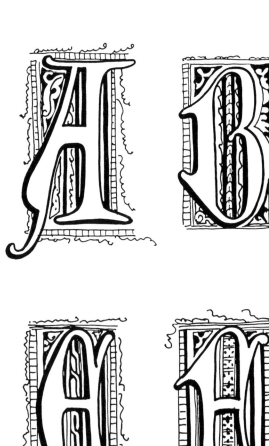  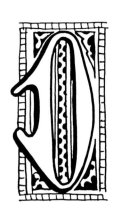
 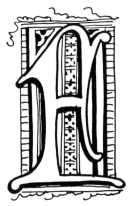  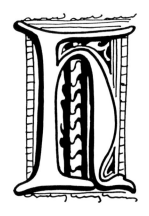
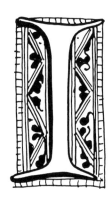 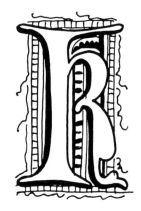 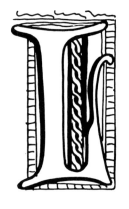 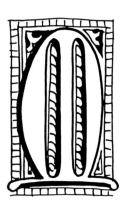

ALPHABETS

INITIALS

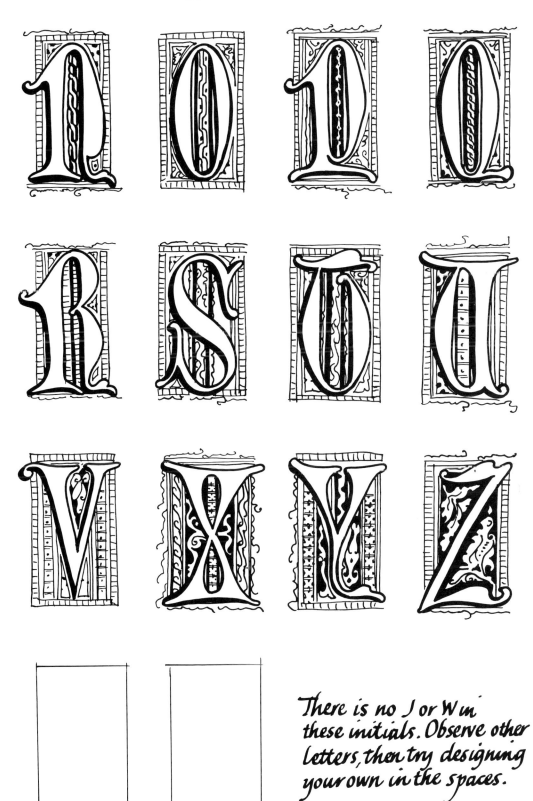

There is no J or W in these initials. Observe other letters, then try designing your own in the spaces.

BACKGROUND DESIGN

Filling in a background is a lot easier than you think. Actually, it's a bit like doodling really - before you realise it, you've designed a whole new letter!

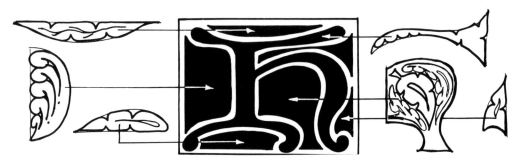

No matter which letter you decide to design, there will always be some regular or irregular space left in the background. You can adapt most of the patterns to fit the spaces.

If you look closely at the decorated letters preceding this page, you will find these designs somewhere in the shapes.

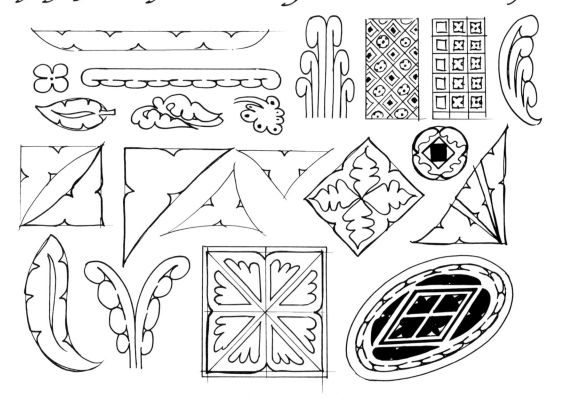

ALPHABETS

BORDERS

Pen borders are simple and easy to do. They are an effective way of finishing off a piece of work.

KNOTS

Because Celtic knots are so symmetrical, graph paper is ideal for this exercise.

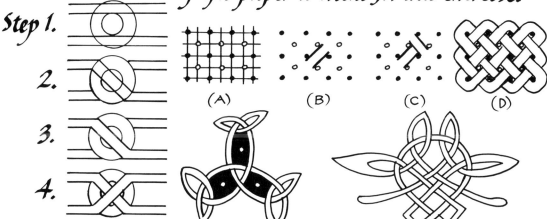

(Based on knotwork from The Book of Kells)

half uncial

Half uncial is based on letters written in Tours (France) in the 9th century.

The letters j, k, s, v and w have been invented.

The long s or ſ should not be confused with the f because the f has a crossbar.

leave a large space between your lines

of writing. as with carolingian this

gives a feeling of openess to the page.

Think majuscules when writing, not minuscules.

Textura

abcdefghijklmno

pqrstuvwxyz

Commonly referred to as "Old English", Textura is the most well-known form of Gothic otherwise known as Black Letter. It was developed in the 12th century from Carolingian, (see page   ) which was written greatly compressed.

ABCDEFGH

IJKLMNOP

RSTUVWQ

XYZ

ALPHABETS

Gothic Cursive

Here is a lesser known Gothic cursive alphabet.

2½ / 3½ a b c d e f g h i j k l m n o p q r

s t u v w x y y y z (& f *Variations of ampersand and the letter f*)

6 A B C D E F G H I J K

L M N O P Q R S T U

V W X Y Z Y Z

The labour of the writer is the refreshment of the reader. The one depletes the body, the other advances the mind. Whoever you are, therefore, do not scorn but be mindful of the work of one labouring to bring you profit. If you do not know how to write you will consider it no hardship.

Rotunda

Rotunda is a style that evolved from Gothic Script, but is much more rounded, hence its name. It was developed in Spain (13th c.).

2/4 abcdefghijklmn
opqrstuvwxyz
adeffgr (Variations of a, d, e, f, g and r)

6 ABCDEFGHI
JKLMNOPQ
RSTUVWXY
3 variations BDVDD
EEEhPQR

Rotunda was commonly used in Books of Hours (personal prayer books), in gigantic manuscripts for church use and in musical notation.

Tempora mutantur et nos mutamur in illis.
Times change, and we change with them.   — EMPEROR LOTHAR (795 - 855 AD)

ALPHABETS

Schwabacher

abcdefghijklmn

opqrstuvwxyz

This style was developed in the early 1470s in Germany. It has a much more rugged character than Fraktur or Textura. (see page 21)

ABCDEFGH

IJKLMNOP

QRSTUVW

XYZ

Bâtarde
14th–16th century

abcdefghijklmn
opqrstuvwxyz

ABCDEF
GHIJKLM
NOPQRS
TUVWXYZ

Scribere qui nescit nullam
putat esse laborum.

Bastard

A modern version of Gothic from the 16th century.

a b c d e f g h i j k

l m n o p q r s t u

v w x y z

A B C D E F G

H I J K L M

O P Q R S T

U V W X Y Z

Fraktur

This hand is a German development of the Gothic letter. It became less popular in the 16th and 17th centuries when pen flourishes and scrollwork became overdone.

abcdefghijklmnop

qrstuvwxyz

adfghs *Variations of lower case*

ABCDEFGH

IJKLMNO

PQRSTUV

WXYZS *Variation*

ALPHABETS
27

Pointed Italic

This style has similar features as that of Chancery Cursive and Black Letter.

abcdefghijklmn

opqrstuvwxyz

ABCDEFG
HIJKLMN
OPQRSTU
VWXYZ

Pointed Italic can also be written upright.
The calligrapher is only concerned with making beautiful forms. ARNOLD BANK

ALPHABETS

Gothic Numerals

1234567890

1234567890

1234567890

Ampersands et et & &

the ampersand evolved from "et",
the Latin word for "and".

& & & & & &

& & & & & &

ALPHABETS

Italic Hand

abcdefghijklmnopq
rstuvwxyz

ABCDEFGHIJKLM
NOPQRSTUVWXYZ

Formal Italic

abcdefghijklmnopq
rstuvwxyz

ABCDEFGHIJKL
MNOPQRSTUVW
XYZ

Maintain a 45° nib angle to the base line.
Watch slope. Use slope lines if necessary.

Chancery Cursive

abcdefghijklmno

pen angle is 45°

pqrstuvwxyz gyyp

variations of lower case

NOTE: Capitals in this style are only 7 pen widths high.

ABCDEFGHIJK

LMNOPQRST

UVWXYZ Maintain a constant slope at all times.

Numerals are always the same height as capitals.

1234567890 & The

In time, with practice, you will write this quite rapidly.

ALPHABETS

Italic Capitals

The lower alphabet is better suited for flourishing.

ABCDEFG
HIJKLMNO
PQRSTUVW
XYZ &

ABCDEFGHIJ
KLMNOPQRST
UVWXYZ &

Italic Capitals

These capitals are ideal for flourishing.

ABCDEFGHI
JKLMNOPQR
STUVWXYZ

ABCDEFG
HIJKLMNO
PPQRSTU
VWXYZ

Flourishes

Flourishes can be used for greater impact in many instances, however - don't overdo them. A flourish is meant to enhance and beautify a letter or word. Too much can render your work illegible.

For example: to finish off a line,

Letters with ascending strokes:

Letters with descending strokes:

Letter combinations:

Flourishing

Cursive or italic capitals are suitable for flourishing.

A A A A A A
B B B B B B
C C D D D D D
D E E E F F
G G G G H H H
I I I J J K K K
K K L L L M M
M M M M M M
N N N N N O O P
P Q Q R R R S
T T T U U V V
W W X Y Y Z Z

ALPHABETS

Copperplate

Copperplate, Engravers script, English roundhand. Also called Spencerian, in honour of one of the finest copperplate engravers of the 18th century, Platt Rogers Spencer.

abcdefghijklmnopqrstuvwxyz

abcdefghijklmnopqrstuvwxyz

AABBCDEE
FFGGHHIJJK
KKLLMMMNN
OPPQQRRSS
TUUVVWXYZ

Copperplate

There are many variations of Copperplate letters, here are just a few.

𝒜 A B C D E
F F G G H H I
J K L L M M
N N O P P Q
R R S T T U
U V V W X Y Y
Z Z

Numerals

1 2 3 4 5 6 7 8 9 0 1 2 3 4

Bookhand
pen widths

4
5
3

a a b c d e f g g h i
j k l m n o p q r s s
t u v w x y y z ✦

9

A B B C D E F F G
H I J K L M N O
P Q R S T U V
W X Y Z &

ALPHABETS
38

Legende

This style is based on the typeface Legend, originally designed by Ernst Schneidler.

a b c d e f g h i j
k l m n o p q r s t u
v w x y z z

A B C D E F G H I J
K L M N O P Q
R S T U V W
X Y Z

ALPHABETS

Foundational Hand

Same technique as for Bookhand.
Note bracketed serifs.

abcdefghijk
lmnopqrstuv
wxyz

Foundational Hand was designed by Edward Johnston and is based on 10th century English roundhand.

ABCDEFG
HIJKLMNO
PQRSTUV
WXYZ
1234567890

Ondine

Based on a typeface of the same name.

abcdefghijkl
mnopqrstuvw
xyzffflfi&

ABCDEEFG
HIJKLMNNO
PQRSTUVV
WXYZ 12345
67890

ALPHABETS

Shamrock

Based on a typeface, originally designed by Alan Withers.

aabcdeFfgh

ijklmnopqrstu

vwxyz &

ABCDEFGHI

JKLMNOPQR

STUVWXYZ

1234567890

Applications

- ENVELOPES
- GREETING CARDS
- SCROLLS
- FANS
- MANUSCRIPT BOOKS

Envelopes AND HOW TO MAKE THEM

Remember to make your envelopes a few mm's larger than the cards. Use a glue stick to glue down the edges. Make a template slightly bigger than your card to speed up the folding of the envelopes.

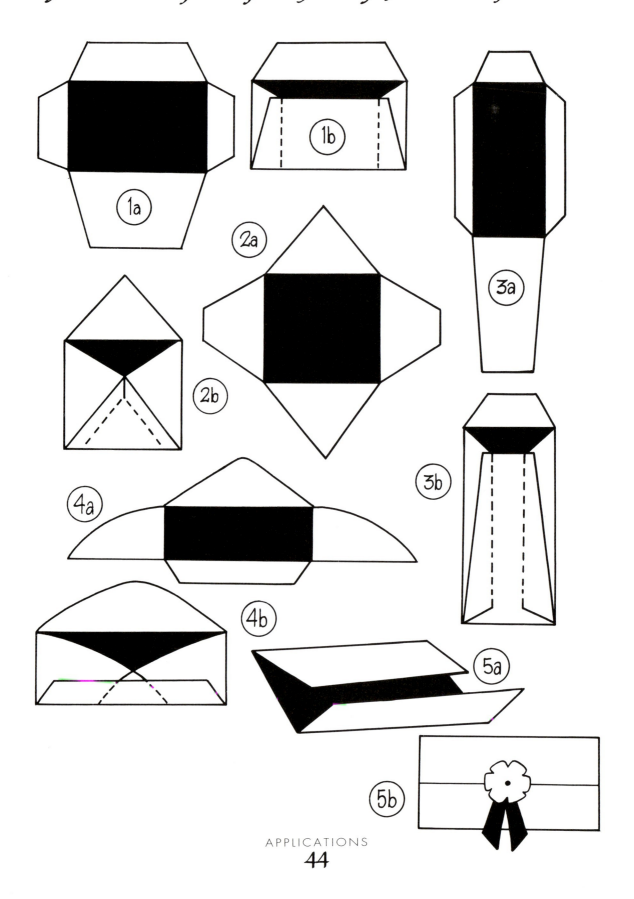

APPLICATIONS
44

Greeting Cards · HOW TO FOLD

Handmade cards are more appreciated by the recipient and can save you heaps of money. If you use a polished board for your card, score along the fold line with a craft knife before folding. This prevents "cracking".

Usual paper size is A4.

NOTE:
If you make your own cards, buy the envelopes to match first.

Scrolls

We have been writing on scrolls for almost 4500 years. Today they are mainly used for commemorative documents and are ideal for long poems and name meanings. You will need a large sheet of parchment and ribbon. The amount of copy will determine the size of the scroll.

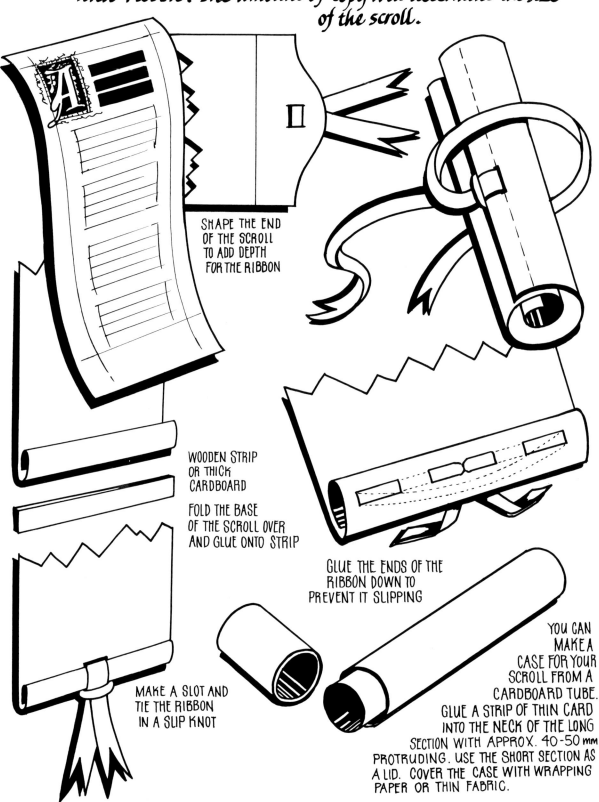

SHAPE THE END OF THE SCROLL TO ADD DEPTH FOR THE RIBBON

WOODEN STRIP OR THICK CARDBOARD

FOLD THE BASE OF THE SCROLL OVER AND GLUE ONTO STRIP

GLUE THE ENDS OF THE RIBBON DOWN TO PREVENT IT SLIPPING

MAKE A SLOT AND TIE THE RIBBON IN A SLIP KNOT

YOU CAN MAKE A CASE FOR YOUR SCROLL FROM A CARDBOARD TUBE. GLUE A STRIP OF THIN CARD INTO THE NECK OF THE LONG SECTION WITH APPROX. 40-50 mm PROTRUDING. USE THE SHORT SECTION AS A LID. COVER THE CASE WITH WRAPPING PAPER OR THIN FABRIC.

Fans

This is a challenging exercise and will test your patience and skills. Because the paper used in fans is quite porous, you will need to use gouache to prevent bleeding. You can also use a felt pen or a color brush.

Commencing from the left side of the fan, write on every second section. Alternate the colour of ink to make the finished job more interesting. Make sure your copy will fit and you won't run out of room.

Manuscript Books

There are a few different ways to bind your calligraphy into a permanent cover. You should plan this before you start your work as you need to fold it into sections. Long poems or riddles are ideal for manuscript books. You will need cardboard approx. 2mm thick for the cover and wrapping paper or thin fabric for the covering. Ribbons of all colours, textures and widths are available for ties. Also needed is a bodkin (a large needle with a blunt end), a bookbinder's needle and some strong thread or a heavy glazed cotton, preferably to match the paper in your book.

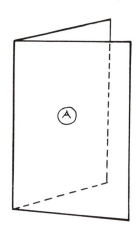 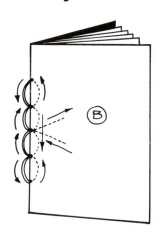 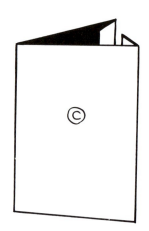

(A) REPRESENTS A FOLDED SINGLE SECTION

(B) USE THIS METHOD TO STITCH ALL SECTIONS TOGETHER

(C) THE MOST BASIC METHOD USED TO COVER A BOOK

NOTE: TIE THE ENDS OF THE THREAD IN A REEF KNOT

Don't write on the first and back page of the folded section. These are the "end papers" and should be glued down onto the cover. This is what holds the pages into the cover.

Don't make the page section too thick or the book won't close.

MAKE THE ACTUAL COVER OF THE BOOK A FEW mm'S LARGER THAN THE PAGES

Manuscript Books

Concertina or accordion manuscript books are very effective and easy to make. You will need a full sheet of parchment or paper, rather than from a pad and some card for the front and back covers.

COVER THE END BOARDS FIRST

CUT A SLIT IN THE COVER, THEN THREAD THE RIBBON OR TAPE THROUGH, USING THE BODKIN

AS WITH THE COVER OF THE MANUSCRIPT BOOK, MAKE THE ENDS BIGGER THAN THE PAGES

Another way of "dressing up" the cover of a book is to weave fancy ribbon through it before putting the stitched section in. Use a plain paper or fabric for the cover to contrast with the ribbon.

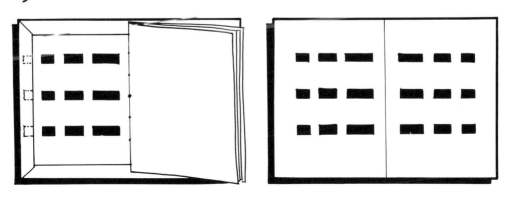

APPLICATIONS

Ready Reference to Line Heights

UNCIAL — 3½

Carolingian — 4 / 2

half uncial — 3 / 2

Gothic
Schwabacher · Textura · Rotunda — 2 / 4
Fraktur — 5 / 6
Bâtarde — 2 / 2
Bastard — 3 / 4
Gothic Cursive

Chancery Cursive — 5 / 5 / 5

5 PEN WIDTHS FOR LOWER CASE – 7 FOR CAPITALS

The same rule also applies to the following styles

Italic Hand · Formal Italic · Pointed Italic

Ready Reference to Line Heights

Copperplate

The copperplate nib is pointed, not square. The line ratio for this style is one third for minuscules and two thirds for majuscules.

Bookhand · Foundational Hand

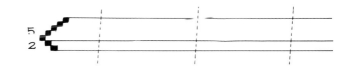

Legende

Ondine

Shamrock

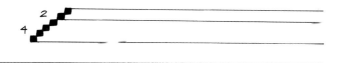

The following are details of Calligraphy Societies in Australia and New Zealand.

Australian Society of Calligraphers Inc.
P.O. BOX 184
WEST RYDE. N.S.W. 2114

Calligraphy Society of Victoria Inc.
BOX 2623W G.P.O.
MELBOURNE. VICTORIA. 3001

Calligraphy Society of South Australia Inc.
P.O. BOX 3114
GRENFELL STREET
ADELAIDE. SOUTH AUSTRALIA. 5000

Calligraphy Society of Tasmania
1 BRITANNIA PLACE
BELLERNE. TASMANIA. 7018

Canberra Calligraphy Society
P.O. BOX E336
QUEEN VICTORIA TERRACE
CANBERRA. A.C.T. 2600

Lettering Arts Society of Queensland
P.O. BOX 264
MOOROOKA. QUEENSLAND. 4105

Maroondah Calligraphy Society
C/O 2 LINDEN ROAD
RINGWOOD. VICTORIA. 3134

The Pen Script Society Tasmania
33 MELVILLE STREET
HOBART. TASMANIA. 7000

The Calligraphy Society of New Zealand
P.O. BOX 99. 674 NEWMARKET
AUCKLAND. NEW ZEALAND.

ALPHABETS
FOR
BRUSHES
AND
FELT PENS
SQUEAKERS OR MARKERS

Introduction to Felt Pens

Originally when I was planning this section, I intended to do a critique on each pen as I did in my first book, Step-By-Step Calligraphy for Students and Teachers. However, because there are so many "felt" pens on the market it is not feasible to do a comparison on all the brands available. At last count there were 23 different brands that I could recall. Every day there are new pens being produced for all kinds of purposes, so that designs are superceded very quickly. So instead of pages of pen comparisons I decided to set this section out in alphabets suitable to each type of pen regardless of the brand.

Although many felt pens are designed for graphic artists they can also be utilised for lettering. In fact anyone, either employer or employee, involved in small business, major retail stores, clubs, theatres etc. who has a need to write quick tickets, showcards, banners, posters, even letter-box flyers will find that brush and pen lettering skills can help increase trade.

Therefore you will need to be able to identify various types of "nib" ends.

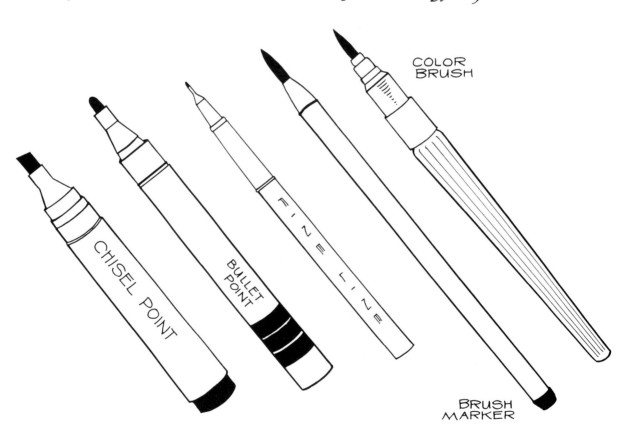

NOTE: PENS HAVE BEEN REDUCED. NOT ACTUAL SIZE.

TYPES:
- BULLET POINT *(usually felt)*
- CHISEL POINT *(felt / fibre or plastic)*
- FINE LINE *(fibre)*
- BRUSH MARKER *(felt or rubber)*
- BRUSH *(not a felt/fibre end but synthetic hair)*

BRANDS:
- ARTLINE
- EDDING
- PILOT
- UNI·POSCA
- STAEDTLER
- MARVY
- BEROL
- SANDFORD
- PLATIGNUM
- SPEEDBALL
- FABER-CASTELL
- SCHWAN STABILO
- PANTONE TRIA
- PENLINE
- SAKURA
- PENTEL
- PELIKAN PLAKA
- COPIC
- YOKEN
- MARUZEN
- NIKKO
- TEXTA

FEATURES: DYES / INKS / TEMPERA

Most brands use all of these mediums in their various pens. It depends what the job is at hand as to which you will need. Tempera is paint and is opaque. Mediums can be any of these:

- WATERPROOF / NON·WATERPROOF
- PERMANENT / NON·PERMANENT / WATER SOLUBLE
- LIGHTFAST or FADEPROOF
- LIMITED LIGHTFASTNESS
- TRANSPARENT / OPAQUE

CAN BE USED ON: PAPER / CARDBOARD / GLASS / METAL / FABRIC

NOTE: You will need to read the side of each pen to determine what uses it has and whether it is suitable for your purposes. BE WARNED! most pens contain quick-drying agents and can cause headaches and sometimes nausea if used for a long period in an enclosed area. Buy pens that are XYLENE FREE and ventilate your work area. Also, if your hands are sweaty, even though your work appears dry, some inks can still smudge. Keep a towel handy or better still wear cotton gloves.

INTRODUCTION TO FELT PENS

MARKERS

Artline DRAWING SYSTEM
0.1 0.2 0.3 0.4 0.6 0.8

STAEDTLER mars *graphic* 0.5 PIGMENT LINER

MARVY OHP MARKER

SAKURA MICRON PIGMA 0.1

Artline 200 0.4 FINE

SAKURA SLIM WRITER

PENTEL Sign PEN

Schwan STABILO point

Artline 210 0.6

SAKURA PEN·TOUCH F

SAKURA CALLIPEN

Osmiroid CALLIGRAPHY B3

Sakura SKETCH PEN

PENLINE

CALLIGRAPHY PEN

PENTEL Calligraphy Pen

ALL PENS ACTUAL SIZE

INTRODUCTION TO FELT PENS

MARKERS and BRUSHES

BULLET POINTS

Artline 70

PENTEL *Stylo* JAPONAIS
RUBBER BRUSH

ARTLINE TEMPERA 4mm
SIGNMARKER

Sakura PEN TOUCH M

Artline 90

CHISEL POINTS

PENLINE
CHISEL POINT

PENTEL
COLOR BRUSH

BRUSHES

FABER-CASTELL

Studiomarker

SAKURA *Sumi Brush*
PIGMA

ALL PENS ACTUAL SIZE

EXAMPLES OF MARKERS & BRUSHES

MARKING PEN SYSTEM or "POTS"

THIS PEN SYSTEM IS USED MAINLY IN LIQUOR STORES, FRUIT SHOPS, BUTCHERIES AND SUPERMARKETS. THEY ARE DESIGNED FOR VERY LARGE POSTERS AND BANNERS. THE "POT" OR PEN CONTAINER IS REFILLABLE WITH AN INK WHICH DRIES IMMEDIATELY. THE PENS ARE OF VARIOUS WIDTHS AND THE FELT LONG-LASTING AND REPLACEABLE. THE PEN POT WILL LAST INDEFINITELY IF CARE IS TAKEN TO ENSURE THE INK DOESN'T DRY UP. TO GET THE BEST PERFORMANCE FROM THESE PENS THEY MUST ALWAYS BE MOIST. THEY WRITE MUCH BETTER ON A SMOOTH SURFACE: CARDBOARD OR POLISHED PAPER. BECAUSE OF THE BULKINESS OF THE LARGER SIZE PENS, THEY CAN BE AWKWARD AND DIFFICULT TO WRITE WITH. THERE ARE A FEW TRICKS IN HOLDING AND USING THEM, SO A FEW FORMAL LESSONS ARE ADVISED.

AVAILABLE IN 6 COLOURS, THIS BRAND FEATURES 3 AND 4 PEN POTS.

MARKETED BY PROMART INTERNATIONAL. THERE ARE OTHER BRANDS, ALTHOUGH THIS IS THE ONLY ONE I HAVE PERSONALLY TRIED.

EXAMPLES OF MARKERS & BRUSHES

EXAMPLES OF MARKERS & BRUSHES

Alphabet Directory

Alphabet Directory

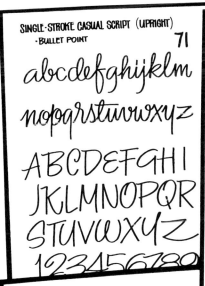

DIRECTORIES
61

SINGLE·STROKE BLOCK CAPITALS & NUMERALS
• BULLET POINT

ABCDEFGHIJ
KLMNOPQRS
TUVWXYZ
1234567890

• BULLET POINT (ITALICS)

ABCDEFGHIJK
LMNOPQRSTUV
WXYZ 12345678

WRITTEN WITH AN ARTLINE 70 PEN

SINGLE·STROKE CAPS & LOWER CASE
• BULLET POINT

ABCDEFGHI
JKLLMNNOP
QRSTUVWX
YZZ &

BASED ON THE TYPEFACE SQUIRE BY MICHAEL NEUGEBAUER

abcdeffghijk
lmnopqrstuv
vwwxyzz
1234567890

WRITTEN WITH A SAKURA PEN·TOUCH F PERMANENT MARKER

SINGLE-STROKE CAPITALS
• BULLET POINT

ABCDEFGHIJKL
MNOPQRSTUV
WXYZ1234567
8990 & $

BASED ON THE STYLE ENVIRO
BY F. SCOTT GARLAND

• BULLET POINT PEN

ABCDEFGHIJ
KLMNOPQR
STUVWXYZ
1234567890 &

STYLED AFTER THE TYPEFACE HARVEY
BY DALE R. KRAMER

WRITTEN WITH A PENTEL SIGN PEN

SINGLE·STROKE CAPITALS, LOWER CASE & NUMERALS

• BULLET POINT

ABCDEFGHIJKL
MNOPQRSTUVW
XYZ&123456789

• BULLET POINT

ABCDEFGHIJ
KLMNOPQRST
UVWXYZ12345
67890abcdefghijk
lmnopqrstuvwxyz

WRITTEN WITH AN ARTLINE 70

SINGLE·STROKE CAPITALS, LOWER CASE & NUMERALS

·BULLET POINT WRITTEN WITH AN ARTLINE 70

ABCDEFGHIJ
KLMNOPQR
STUVWXYZ&
abcdefghijklm
nopqrstuvwxyz
1234567890

·BULLET POINT BASED ON A STYLE DESDEMONA

ABCDEFGHI
JKLMNOPQRS
TUVWXYZ 123
4567890

WRITTEN WITH AN ARTLINE
SIGNMARKER 4mm TEMPERA
WATERPROOF, WATER-BASED
WATERPROOF AND FADEPROOF.

ALPHABETS

SINGLE-STROKE CONDENSED CAPITALS, LOWER CASE
• FINE POINT

ABCDEFGHIJKLMNOP
QRSTUVWXYZ &
abcdefghijklmnopqrstuv
wxyz 1234567890

WRITTEN WITH AN ARTLINE 200, 0·4

• FINE POINT

ABCDEFGHIJKLM
NOPQRSTUVWXYZ
1234567890

WRITTEN WITH A SAKURA SLIM WRITER

TYPES OF SCRIPT

BASICALLY THERE ARE ONLY FOUR TYPES ON WHICH SCRIPT IS STYLED. SCRIPT CAN BE AN EXTENSION OF YOUR OWN HANDWRITING, SO STYLES CAN VARY FROM ONE WRITER TO ANOTHER. ALL OF THESE SCRIPTS CAN BE WRITTEN WITH A PEN OR BRUSH.

simple script

WRITTEN WITH A PENLINE FELT CALLIGRAPHY PEN

Copperplate

SEE REFERENCE FOR COPPERPLATE IN THE CALLIGRAPHY SECTION

WRITTEN WITH A WILLIAM MITCHELL COPPERPLATE PEN

Casual Script

WRITTEN WITH A PENTEL COLOR BRUSH

Built-up script

BASIC SHAPE WRITTEN WITH A SAKURA PEN-TOUCH F
BUILT-UP WITH A SAKURA SLIM WRITER

ALPHABETS

CASUAL SCRIPT BRUSH

MORE WEIGHT ON HEAVY STROKES FOR BUILT-UP
WRITTEN WITH A FABER-CASTELL STUDIOMARKER
TOUCHED-UP WITH AN ARTLINE DRAWING SYSTEM PEN 0.2

abcdefghijkl
mnopqrstuvw
xyz ABCDE
FGHIJKL
MNOPQRS
TUVWXYZ

SINGLE-STROKE CASUAL SCRIPT (SLOPED)
• BULLET POINT

abcdefghijklm
nopqrstuvwxyz

ABCDEFG
HIJKLM
NOPQRST
UVWXYZ

ARTLINE 70

SINGLE-STROKE CASUAL SCRIPT (UPRIGHT)
• BULLET POINT

abcdefghijklm
nopqrstuvwxyz

ABCDEFGHI
JKLMNOPQR
STUVWXYZ
123456789

WRITTEN WITH A SAKURA PEN-TOUCH F

SINGLE·STROKE *ITALIC* CAPITALS & NUMERALS
• CHISEL END

THIS ALPHABET IS WRITTEN WITH THE PEN HELD AT A 45° ANGLE TO THE GUIDE LINES. KEEP THE PEN TIP FLAT ON THE PAPER TO AVOID RAGGED PEN STROKES.

ABBCDDEF
GHIJKLMN
OPPQRRST
UVWXYYZ
1234567890

WRITTEN WITH A NOUVEL DESIGN MARKER BY SAKURA

ALPHABETS

SINGLE·STROKE *ITALIC* Lowercase
• CHISEL END

aabcdefgg
hijkkImnop
qrstuvwxyz

SLOPE REMAINS CONSTANT
REGARDLESS OF LINE ANGLE OR DIRECTION

ITALIC LETTERS ARE EASY!

BRUSHES SUITABLE FOR LETTERING

FOR BRUSH ALPHABETS (THOSE OF A CASUAL STYLE) THE BRANDS FEATURED ARE THOSE I HAVE PERSONALLY ADAPTED FOR LETTERING. THERE ARE PROBABLY MANY OTHERS EQUALLY AS GOOD.

- NOTE: THE WEIGHT OF THE LETTERS DEPENDS ENTIRELY ON THE PRESSURE APPLIED TO BRUSH STROKES.

- FABER-CASTELL STUDIOMARKER

- STAEDTLER MARS GRAPHIC 3000 DUO

- SAKURA PIGMA SUMI BRUSH (DOUBLE-ENDED)

- PENTEL COLOR BRUSH (SYNTHETIC HAIR, INK CARTRIDGE)

ALPHABETS

SINGLE·STROKE *ITALIC* CAPITALS & NUMERALS
· BRUSH

ABBCDDEFG
HIJKKLMN
OPPQRRSS
TUVWXYYZ
123456789

WRITTEN WITH A PENTEL COLOR BRUSH

SINGLE·STROKE CAPITALS & NUMERALS
· BRUSH

ABBCDDEFG
HIJKKLMNO
PPQRRSTU
VWXYYZ&
1234567890

WRITTEN WITH A PENTEL COLOR BRUSH

SINGLE-STROKE LOWER CASE
• BRUSH

aabcdefgg

hijkklmnop

qrsttuvwx

WRITTEN WITH A PENTEL COLOR BRUSH

yyz · casual

upright or

sloping

ALPHABETS

CASUAL THICK AND THIN BLOCK
• BRUSH MARKER

ABCDEFG
HIJKLMN
OPQRSTU
VWXYZ
1234567
890

WRITTEN WITH A FABER-CASTELL
STUDIO MARKER

SERIFS

sĕrĭf noun (Typography) Cross-line finishing off a stroke of a letter as in T (compare SANSERIF T) [perhaps from Dutch *schreef* dash, line from Germanic *skrebh-*] OXFORD DICTIONARY

THE ENTIRE APPEARANCE AND CHARACTER OF A LETTER CAN BE CHANGED VERY SIMPLY BY ADDING A SERIF. A SERIF IS ONLY ANOTHER FORM OF DECORATION AND SHOULD NOT OVERPOWER THE LETTER, SO KEEP IT SIMPLE.

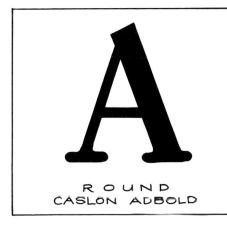

ROUND
CASLON ADBOLD

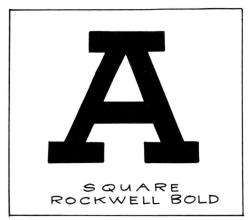

SQUARE
ROCKWELL BOLD

POINTED
TIFFANY HEAVY

TRIANGULAR
CORTEZ

CALLIGRAPHIC
BOOKHAND

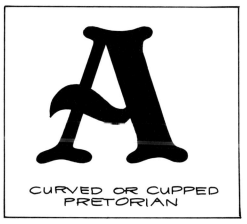

CURVED OR CUPPED
PRETORIAN

ALL STYLES (EXCEPT BOOKHAND)
ARE LETRASET

ALPHABETS

OUTLINING IS ONLY A DECORATION AND SHOULD BE KEPT LIGHT IN WEIGHT

ALWAYS KEEP LETTERS CLOSE TOGETHER FOR OUTLINING

ANY ALPHABET WITH A HEAVY PEN STROKE CAN BE OUTLINED

BDJMQVXZ
123456789

WRITTEN AND OUTLINED WITH A NOUVEL DESIGN MARKER (DUAL TIPPED)

THE CLASSIC ROMAN ALPHABET

No lettering book would be complete without the Classic Roman alphabet. The most well-known inscription is without doubt that on the base of the Trajan column in Rome, incised into the stone about 114 BC. These letters represent at least 700 years of development. The letters H, J, K, U, W, Y and Z do not appear on the Trajan column. They have been added into the alphabet to tie in with the style of the other letters.

Lettering designers of the Renaissance period, Leonardo da Vinci, Geofroy Tory, Moyllus and Albrecht Durer all used geometrical methods to design Classic Roman letters. Featured here are those of Albrecht Durer. I know of no reason to alter or tamper with his exceptional work, therefore it is just as he designed it almost 500 years ago.

"... and first, for the Roman letters: Draw for each a square of uniform size, in which the letter is to be contained. But when you draw in it the heavier limb of the letter, make this of the width of a tenth part of the square, and the lighter a third as wide as the heavier: and follow this rule for all the letters of the Alphabet."

from the APPLIED GEOMETRY OF
ALBRECHT DURER 1525

CLASSIC ROMAN — Albrecht Durer · 1525

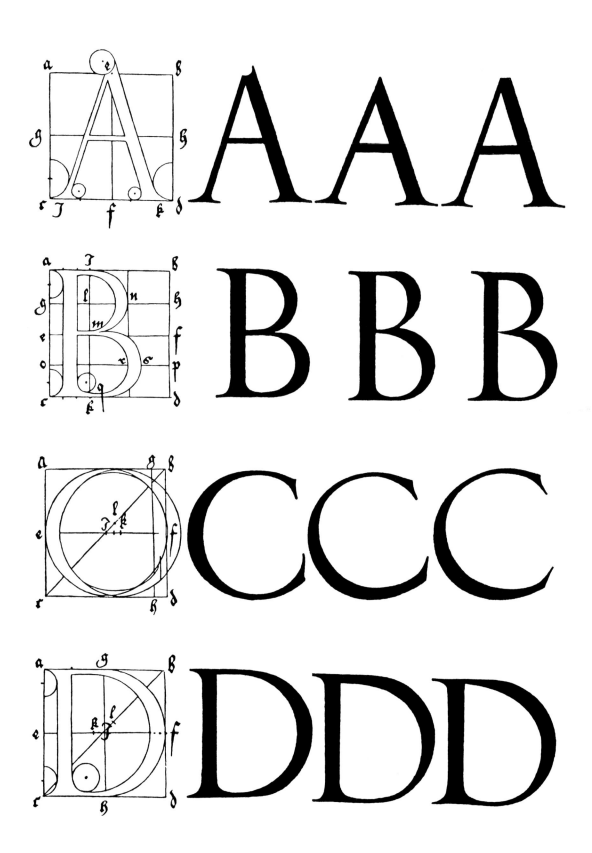

CLASSIC ROMAN — Albrecht Durer · 1525

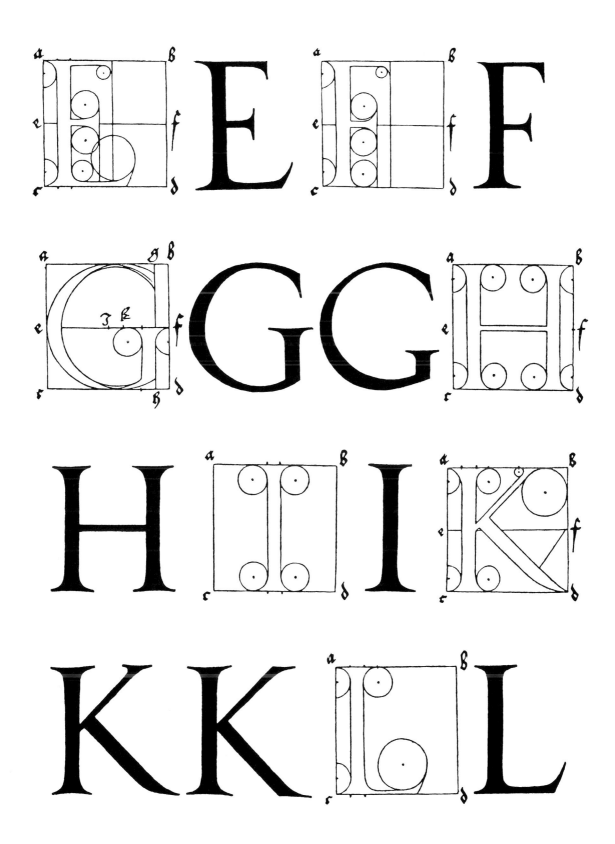

CLASSIC ROMAN   *Albrecht Dürer - 1525*

CLASSIC ROMAN — Albrecht Durer - 1525

CLASSIC ROMAN *Albrecht Durer · 1525*

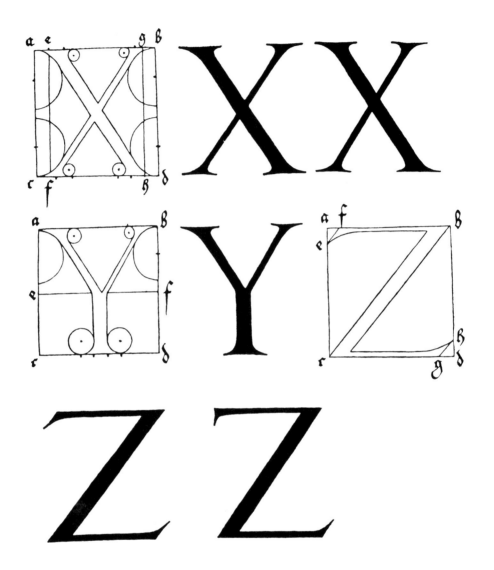

ALPHABETS
86

ADAPTING TYPEFACE FOR FELT PENS

BE AWARE THAT TYPEFACE OR FONTS ARE DRAWN, NOT LETTERED DIRECTLY. THAT IS, A DESIGNER OF ALPHABETS OR A TYPOGRAPHER ACTUALLY DRAWS EACH LETTER AND THEN FILLS IT IN WHEN THEY ARE SATISFIED WITH THE FINAL SHAPE. LETTERS ARE DRAWN MUCH LARGER THAN THE REQUIRED SIZE AND PHOTOGRAPHICALLY REDUCED.

ON SOME OF THE ALPHABETS FEATURED IN THIS BOOK, YOU WILL NOTICE THAT THEY HAVE BEEN BASED, ADAPTED OR STYLED ON VARIOUS TYPEFACES. YOU MAY FIND A STYLE YOU WOULD LIKE TO USE IN ONE OF THE DRY OR RUB-DOWN LETTERING CATALOGUES (LETRASET, RAPITYPE, GEOTYPE ETC.) BUT YOU WILL HAVE TO ADAPT IT TO THE WRITING TOOL YOU INTEND USING.

USING THE STYLE YOU HAVE CHOSEN, WRITE THE BASIC SHAPE.

WITH A FINER PEN, DRAW IN THE AREAS TO BE BUILT-UP.

FILL IN WITH A MEDIUM NIB OR THE FINELINE PEN.

ORNAMENTAL ROMAN

ABCDEF
GHIJKL
MNOPQ
RSTUVW
XYZ

BASIC SHAPE, PENTEL SIGN PEN
FILL-IN, ARTLINE 200 0·4

abcdefghi
jklmnopqr
stuvwxyz

FREE-STYLE ROMAN

ABCDE
FGHIJK
LMNOP
QRSTU
VWXY
ZAAA ① ②

① DRAWN IN OUTLINE WITH AN ARTLINE 70
② SERIFS ROUNDED OFF WITH A MARVY OHP MARKER

SHADING

Shading, like serifs and outlining, is another form of decoration. There are 3 types; direct, indirect (or relief) and drop. Which type you use and how heavy you make it will depend on the style of lettering and how much impact you want to convey. Ticketwriters usually shade to the left of a letter, signwriters to the right.

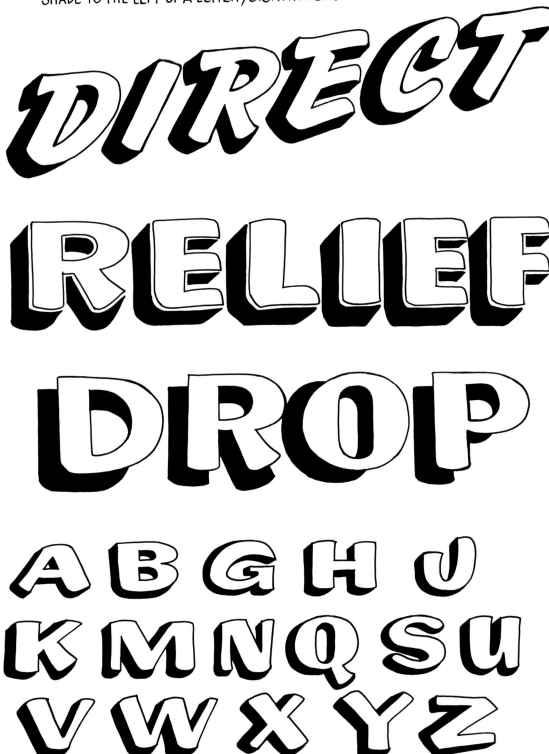

ALPHABETS

Applications

- MENUS/FLYERS
- WINE LISTS/MENU COVERS
- LAYOUT
- TEMPLATES FOR MULTIPLE TICKETING

WINE LISTS / MENU COVERS

ALL CAMERA-READY ART USED IS CLIPPER FROM DYNAMIC GRAPHICS

- DUKES
    - MAIN HEADING, BUILT-UP FREE-STYLE ROMAN
- TIMBERTOWN
    - ALL COPY WRITTEN WITH A WHITE OPAQUE PEN
- GONZALES
    - UPRIGHT CASUAL BLOCK, OTHER COPY BASED ON UNCIAL
- THAI MANIE
    - LETTERING DRAWN FROM LETRASET STYLE ARTISTIK

APPLICATIONS

MENUS/FLYERS

ALWAYS DO A ROUGH PENCIL LAYOUT BEFORE COMMENCING

MENUS / FLYERS

Main headings here are all built-up styles. Roman, script and casual block.

ALL ANCHORS MENUS REPRODUCED WITH KIND PERMISSION OF PETER DAVIS

APPLICATIONS

FLYERS (BROCHURES/DODGERS)

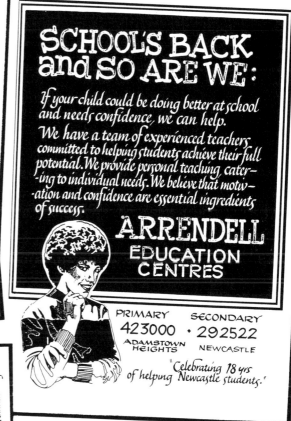

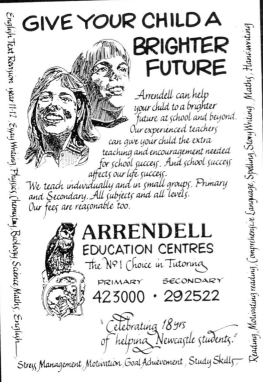

MOST OF THE EXAMPLES FEATURED IN THIS BOOK DEMONSTRATE BOTH FELT PEN AND CALLIGRAPHY SKILLS.

PLACEMENT OF ARTWORK (BROMIDES) IS CRUCIAL. GRAPHICS MUST LEAD THE VIEWER'S EYE INTO THE LAYOUT, NOT OUT.

LAYOUTS REPRODUCED WITH KIND PERMISSION OF GWENDA SANDERSON

APPLICATIONS

LAYOUT

> DEPENDING ON WHERE THE EMPHASIS IS PLACED...

> THE SAME WORDING CAN BE SET OUT IN NUMEROUS WAYS

LAYOUT

TRY AS MANY DIFFERENT WAYS OF SETTING OUT COPY AS YOU CAN, BEFORE DECIDING ON THE FINAL DRAFT.

APPLICATIONS

TEMPLATES for MULTIPLE TICKETING

TICKETWRITERS ARE OFTEN REQUIRED TO WRITE MORE THAN ONE SHOWCARD OR TICKET USING THE SAME LAYOUT AND WORDING. THIS IS KNOWN AS "MULTIPLE TICKETING". THE EASIEST AND MOST TIME-SAVING METHOD IS TO MAKE A TEMPLATE OR PATTERN. THIS ASSISTS GREATLY IN RULING UP AND MAKES A SOMETIMES TEDIOUS JOB MUCH QUICKER. IT ALSO ENSURES THAT EACH TICKET IS IDENTICAL IN STYLE AND LAYOUT.

ON A PIECE OF CARDBOARD, THE SAME SIZE AS THE REQUIRED TICKETS, RULE UP THE LINES AS PER COPY SUPPLIED.

USING A STENCIL OR CRAFT KNIFE, CUT OUT EACH SHAPE TO FORM A "WINDOW" IN TEMPLATE.

THEN RULE UP AS MANY TICKETS AS ARE NEEDED!

APPLICATIONS

Recommended Books

- The Encyclopedia of Calligraphy Techniques · DIANA HARDY WILSON · 1990
- Calligraphy · DAVID HARRIS · RANDOM HOUSE · 1991
- The Calligraphers Dictionary · ROSE FOLSOM · THAMES & HUDSON · 1990
- Writing: The Story of Alphabets & Scripts · GEORGES JEAN · T. & H. · 1992
- Historic Alphabets & Initials · CAROL BELANGER GRAFTON · DOVER · 1977
- Decorative Alphabets & Initials · ALEXANDER NESBITT · DOVER · 1959
- Treasury of Art Nouveau Design & Ornament · C.B. GRAFTON · DOVER · 1980
- Art Nouveau: An Anthology of Design & Illustration · GILLON · DOVER · 1969
- Lettering Techniques · JOHN LANCASTER · ARCO · 1982
- Writing Implements & Accessories · J.I. WHALLEY · DAVID & CHARLES · 1980
- The Calligraphers Project Book · SUSANNE HAINES · COLLINS · 1987
- The Complete Guide to Calligraphy · JUDY MARTIN · PHAIDON · 1984
- Studio Tips · BILL GRAY · DESIGN PRESS · 1978
- More Studio Tips for Artists & Graphic Designers · BILL GRAY · D. PRESS · 1978
- Lettering Tips for Artists, G. Des. & Calligraphers · BILL GRAY · D. PRESS · 1980
- Calligraphy Tips · BILL GRAY · DESIGN PRESS ·
- Tips on Making Greeting Cards · BILL GRAY · DESIGN PRESS · 1991
- Doorposts · TIMOTHY BOTTS · TYNDALE HOUSE · 1987
- Advanced Calligraphy Techniques · DIANA HOARE · CHARTWELL · 1989

Recommended Books

For those interested in the history of lettering—

- Historical Scripts STAN KNIGHT 1984
- The Story of Writing DONALD JACKSON 1981
- The Decorated Letter J. J. G. ALEXANDER 1978
- Books of Hours JOHN HARTHAN 1977
- The Pen's Excellence JOYCE WHALLEY 1980
- The Lindisfarne Gospels JANET BACKHOUSE 1981
- The Book of Kells THAMES & HUDSON 1988
- Illuminated Manuscripts THAMES & HUDSON 1988

Suppliers

I have included only the local suppliers, that I am familiar with. I cannot list stores in other states, they would be too numerous. You have only to look under Artist Supplies in your telephone book for the supplier nearest to you.

My personal thanks to the following three companies. They have always been more than helpful with any requests I have had, whether for myself or for students.

- Eckersley's CNR. UNION & PARRY STS. NEWCASTLE.
  (049) 29 3423 (also in QLD., VIC., & S.A.)
- Our Town Art Supplies 573 HUNTER ST. NEWCASTLE.
  (049) 29 4650
- Will's Quills 164 VICTORIA AVE, CHATSWOOD. SYDNEY.
  (02) 419 2112